This book belongs to:

....

....

GRAFFEG

Animal Surprises
published by Graffeg June 2016
© Copyright Graffeg 2016
ISBN 9781910862445

Text © 2016 Nicola Davies.
Illustrations © 2016 Abbie Cameron.
Designed and produced by Graffeg
www.graffeg.com

Graffeg Limited, 24 Stradey Park Business
Centre, Mwrwg Road, Llangennech, Llanelli,
Carmarthenshire SA14 8YP Wales UK
Tel 01554 824000 www.graffeg.com

Graffeg are hereby identified as the authors of
this work in accordance with section 77 of the
Copyrights, Designs and Patents Act 1988.

A CIP Catalogue record for this book is available
from the British Library.

ANIMAL SURPRISES

Written by
Nicola Davies

Illustrated by
Abbie Cameron

On all the pages
of this book
Are ANIMALS,
So take a look!
Creatures of all
Shapes and sizes,
Some you'll know
and Some...

Some are

big,

some pretty small

Some you can hardly see at all.

Some are skinny as a string,
Some are fat as anything!

Round and Cute and Very furry.

or Spiky,

Scaly, curly whirly.

Creatures of all shapes and sizes,

Some have two legs,

Some have four,

FINDA MINIBEAST

some have six,

or eight

or more!

Animals with none must

Wriggle,

Creep and crawl

and squirm and squiggle.

Some, instead,

have flukes and fins

Or flapping, gliding, zooming wings.

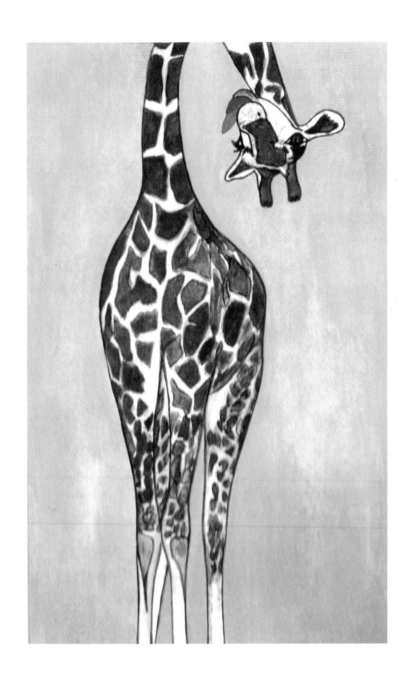

Tall and thin

Or short and squat,

Shaped like a Star

or just a dot.

Creatures of all Shapes and Sizes,

Some you'll know and some...

SURPR

ISES!

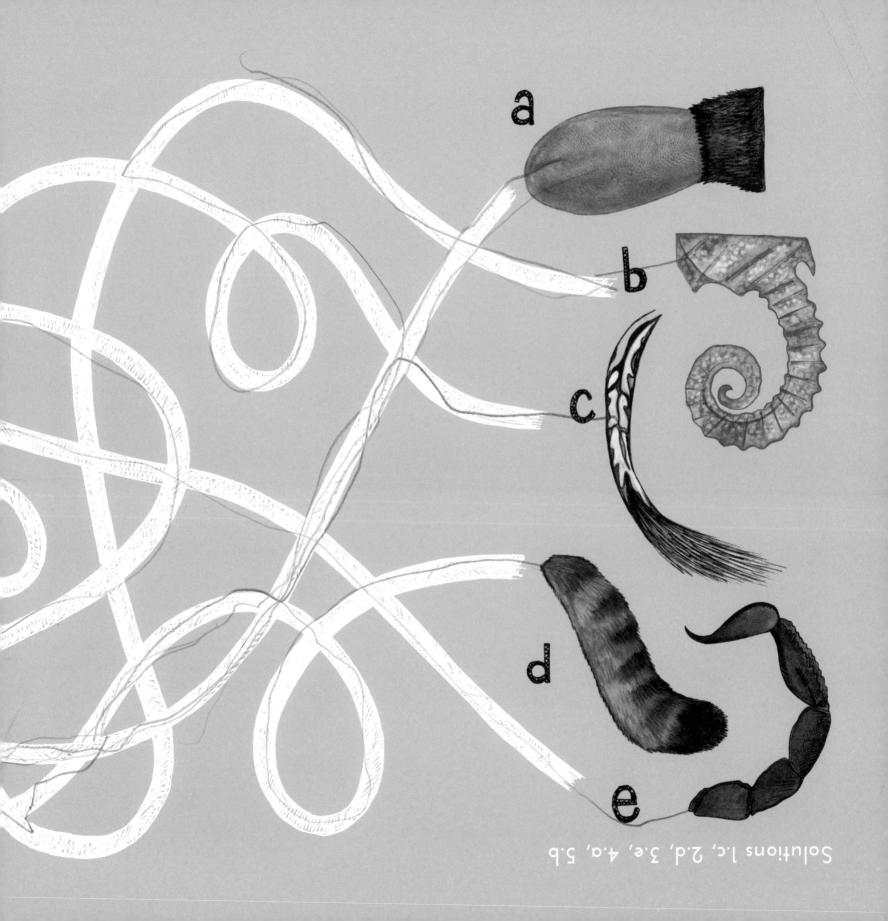

a

b

c

d

e

Solutions 1.c, 2.d, 3.e, 4.a, 5.b

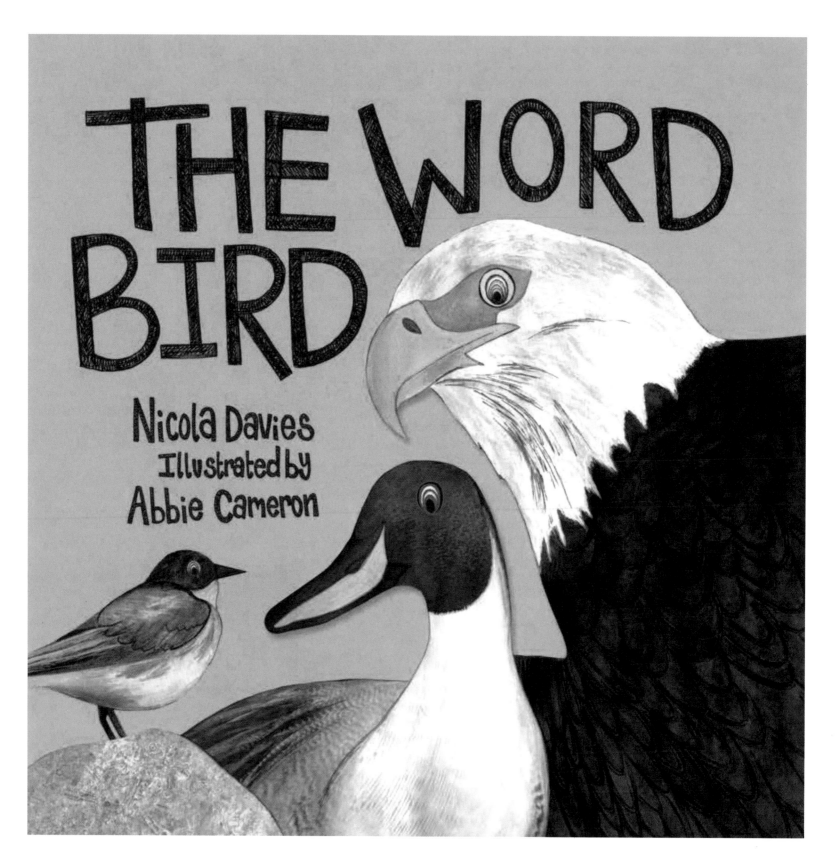

The Word Bird, also available in this series.

Into The Blue, also available in this series.

Nicola Davies

Nicola is an award-winning author, whose many books for children include
The Promise (Green Earth Book Award 2015, Greenaway Shortlist 2015), *Tiny*
(AAAS Subaru Prize 2015), *A First Book of Nature*, *Whale Boy* (Blue Peter Award
Shortlist 2014), and the Heroes of the Wild Series (Portsmouth Book Prize
2014). She graduated in zoology, studied whales and bats and then worked for
the BBC Natural History Unit. Underlying all Nicola's writing is the belief that a
relationship with nature is essential to every human being, and that now, more
than ever, we need to renew that relationship. Nicola's children's books from
Graffeg include *Perfect*, the Shadows and Light series, *The Word Bird*,
Animal Surprises and *Into the Blue*.

Abbie Cameron

Abbie Cameron was raised on the farmlands of the West Country. Surrounded by
nature, she developed a love and appreciation for all creatures great and small.
Abbie studied Illustration at University of Wales Trinity Saint David, where she first
met Nicola Davies. Her style is playful and inventive, sharing some of the tongue-
in-cheek attitude and doodle-like style of other contemporary British illustrators.
She employs the use of bright colours and texture, whilst playing with scale,
composition and open space. *The Word Bird*, *Animal Surprises* and *Into the Blue*
are Abbie's first published books but she hopes to continue a career in picture
book illustration. Other notable achievements include being short-listed and
received highly commented in the Penguin Random House Design Awards 2014.